THE FUGITIVE'S BABY

Kass Ghayouri

ISBN-10: 1482658437

EAN-13: 9781482658439

CreateSpace Independent Publishing Platform

Dedication

This labor of love is dedicated to my sons Omid and Shahrooz

Acknowledgments

First and foremost, I would like to thank my sons, Shahrooz and Omid (my leaves): Thank you for your invaluable contributions to my dream. Your patience and understanding enabled me to spend quality time writing this novel. Indeed, I am exceptionally blessed and fortunate to have your sincere support. You bring me inspiration and a sense of purpose.

I am also indebted to my students for their untiring devotion to promoting my novel. May this novel inspire them to attain their goals. Their enthusiasm was the rain that showered me with inspiration. Special heartwarming thanks to Nishaani, Taanya, and Pavithra for their dedicated and loyal help. I understand their impatient anticipation for this novel. Additionally, I extend my gratitude to all those who helped me in the process of publishing.

CHAPTER 1

The Visitor was a new immigrant to Canada. She arrived at her relatives' house, expecting a bright future. She was a beautiful and elegant young lady with a sophisticated air. She approached the home with a huge warm smile and a twinkle in her eye.

The new Visitor was Indo-Mauritian. She was of Indian origin who lived on the island of Mauritius. She hailed from the Brahmin caste and class. She was from a wealthy family of Gold merchants, who formed the upper class of the Indian society in Mauritius. Her cultural identity was indeed intact. Her cast and class system was more complex. Since she came from a wealthy family, they dominated the economic and political arena of the island. Her family members had the mindset and intelligence that led them to exceptional wealth. The Visitor felt that her parents created her life and as a young adult she was in control of her life. Taking full responsibility of her own life, she wanted to create the life of her dream. She wanted to travel and live in a foreign country, for the sake of adventure. She believed that the universe would conspire to help her. She viewed moving to a foreign country, as an opportunity and not an obstacle. She saw her move as a blessing and a stepping stone to achieve success. She wanted to be the architect of her own wealth. She wanted self respect. Her relatives created the impression that they were enthusiastic about having her as their guest. Julie was charismatic but tortured by her inner demons. Julie often gloated about their life in Canada and encouraged the Visitor to explore career opportunities in a new country. It was nothing but a hyperbole.

However, she did not yet know that the house she was about to enter was a house of horrors. It was an upright wooden house with dried and worn out siding and gaping holes in part of the concrete foundation. The house screamed of neglect. Despite this, she thought a warm welcome and a homely atmosphere may be waiting inside.

But with her first breath inside the house, an eerie feeling closed in on her, causing her skin to tingle. It was like the house was inhabited by disembodied spirits of the dead who had inhabited the home decades before. It felt like the house was possessed. She immediately perceived that this was the phenomena associated with an economically and emotionally troubled house. The Visitor felt her anxiety rise.

A family of four stood unmoving at the door. Julie had a sly smirk. She did not blink or move. She just giggled, in an eerie manner. Her hair was jet-black. Her face was pure white. She seemed to be nervous. Julie, the lady of the household, stood out from the others. She had tried to bleach her dark face with prescription creams, however the effects were devastating. Her bleached face was as pale as a Halloween ghost. Her face glowed in the dim surroundings. It lit up the tarn surroundings.

"We were expecting you," Julie said with a squeaky voice and a Canadian accent. "Come in. You must be hungry," she continued.

As the Visitor entered the dwelling and proceeded to the cluttered kitchen, she heard the old hardwood floors cracking and breaking apart under her. It felt as though she was going to discover an entombed corpse ahead. The crumbling feeling inside her grew, but she could not turn back.

Julie's husband, Dan, ushered the Visitor to a chair. "Sit down. I did not know that you were going to stay with us. I was not informed about having another visitor at our home," he said as his nose wrinkled in between his wide-set eyes.

As he spoke in a chatterbox voice, his polly nose wrinkled in-between his wide set eyes. Immediately, the symbolic decay of a dysfunctional family was exposed. The explicit psychological dimension of a troubled family, with economical discomfort was evident.

"I told you she was coming, Dan. You are so stupid," yelled Julie.

With the same disrespectful tone, their daughter, Shella, echoed her mother as she yelled at her father. "Why don't you shut up? You are such a freakin' fool! Mom told you that she was going to stay with us."

"Your mother is a bloody fool. She is the stupid one in her family…" Dan continued the verbal abuse and brought up all of Julie's psychological problems without pausing.

Their son, Monk, stood silently in a corner with a disturbing grin.

His rectangular shaped face resembled Frankenstein. The Visitor analyzed the situation and knew that the family had a history of evil and cruelty. And she was trapped here. She felt as if she was placed in a family crypt and pledged that some day she would escape such abuse. She promised herself that she would someday escape.

* * *

Months had passed and the Visitor became the target of the family's verbal and psychological abuse. She felt like she was Cinderella, living in a house with the evil stepmother and her angry daughter, Shella. The Visitor was the sole servant to this dysfunctional family. Julie asked her to mend Monks pants, on one particular occasion. The Visitor tried her best. However Julie was not interested in the final outcome. She slammed doors and cussed at the Visitor.

"Now I have to pay a tailor, to get that fixed," she yelled in an obnoxious tone.

"I will fix it!" the Visitor begged.

Another door slammed with a loud bang! That night the visitor slept on a mat, on the floor of the basement. She was given cold pasta and tomato sauce to eat.

Julie's schizophrenia became apparent to the Visitor. Julie often hallucinated and seemed delusional. Her thoughts were disorganized, she didn't concentrate on things, and she was unable to follow instructions. As her depression increased, Julie became paranoid. Her profound disruption in cognition and emotion was evident, and had an impact on her fundamental human attributes. Her behavior ranged from frequent psychotic manifestations to hallucinations and delusions. She began to conjure up stories about the Visitor. Her bizarre behavior was exemplified in the way she slammed doors and constantly threw hints of verbal abuse at her visitor.

"You can do what you want to do. I do not care about you. I hate you. I just love my children," she would rage at the Visitor.

"I am so hungry. I want a cheese sandwich but I cannot afford it."

"I need glasses. You need to buy me eyeglasses. I will not wear any brand of glasses but Calvin Klein."

"Some people in this house wear new clothing…ummmm they buy clothing…I need to tell my brother about this…I hate you…I hate your mother…I hate you."

Julie often yelled out these paranoid delusions of persecution, and claimed that she was physically ill. This was followed by delusions of grandeur, where Julie believed that she had the special powers to kill the new visitor in her home. Her hallucinations became visual, auditory, tactile, olfactory and gustatory.

When the Visitor was near, Julie would engage in a jumbled "word salad," with ongoing disjointed and rambling monologues. The Visitor was often the target of Julie's nagging. Julie would also display catatonic behavior. She hated the Visitor with a passion. All of Julie's frustrations were directed at the Visitor.

To make matters worse, Julie was a kleptomaniac. She had the irresistible urge to steal money from the Visitor's purse every day. Julie was also compelled to steal other items of trivial value with an irresistible urge from the Visitor. Found items like night gowns and night shirts went missing. Julie's stealing became addictive and compulsive. She would steal the Visitor's nightgowns and used nightshirts and hand them over to her poor sister-in-law who lived in the same neighborhood.

Julie's kleptomania was accompanied by a comorbid condition of paranoia, schizoid and borderline personality disorder, which led to her employers firing her from her job.

The day she was fired was like a nightmare to the visitor who had to succumb to such violent verbal abuse. She was fired because she stole large sums of money and trivial office supplies from her employer. In addition, her employer discovered that Julie had a previous police record and prison term for theft.

Life for the visitor, who was waiting for her immigration status in Canada, became hell on earth. She lived in Canada on a work permit. Her adventurous nature prompted her to travel. She was in search of a different experience. Her initial plan was to live in a foreign country for a few years. Experiencing a different culture and country was fascinating. She was scared of living with a schizophrenic relative in a dysfunctional home. She was in a house of horrors and she felt tormented by its flame. She could feel the furnace of fire around her, as Julie continuously engaged in her dramatic monologue or "word salad", hinting at the visitor's mere existence.

To add fuel to the fire, Julie had a regular guest, who was her alcoholic brother, Willy. He lived in the same poverty-stricken and crime ridden neighborhood. His uncontrolled consumption of alcohol led to him being fired from his job, which meant he spent more time at Julie's house. The Visitor was sandwiched in-between a schizophrenic Julie and her chronic alcoholic brother, Willy. She was bombarded from all sides by Julie's and Willy's terrible behavior.

"Hey, little one, I will not rest in peace until I see you six feet underground," rambled the drunken Willy as he addressed the Visitor.

"What did I do to you to deserve such animosity?" she asked in response.

"With people like you around, who needs friends, your very existence disgusts me," he yelled as he approached her. His breath reeked of alcohol. His alcohol dependence syndrome was evident.

"Give me some money. I need money to buy smokes, you slut. Give Julie some money too. My son needs money for college. You need to pay his college tuition fees. My wife needs money for the late mortgage payments. You have money in your bank account. We need that money from you!"

As Willy yelled this, he held the Visitor in a chokehold. The grappling hold could have strangled her. The strangle hold revealed disparity in strength, and she felt as if her airway was being compressed. He was much stronger than her and his hands were like a python constricting her throat. She felt the excruciating pain and hungered for air. She knew that his chokehold would fracture her larynx and she had to struggle to free herself. She thought about her family in her home country and wondered how they would find out about her death. She grabbed onto Willy's biceps. She could not risk passing out from a lack of oxygen. She freed herself. She was in a state of panic. She threatened to call the police. Since Willy had a long record with the police, for domestic violence, he fled like a coward.

The verbal abuse from Julie was psychologically painful. The physical abuse from Willy was dangerous. Dan constantly nagged the Visitor about Julie's lack of interest in sex and her family's greediness. Shella's temper tantrums drove the visitor insane. Willy's wife constantly asked to borrow money from the Visitor. The threatening neighborhood was full of drug addicts, pimps, and prostitutes. All of this was overwhelming.

Once the visitor asked Shella if she wanted to read a magazine. The Visitor was excited when Shella agreed.

"Yes, I would love to read it," she expressed ,with such gratitude.

"Here you go some interesting articles!"the Visitor exclaimed.

"Bring it to me," said Shella with a broad smile.

The Visitor entered the room and handed the magazine to Shella. The Visitor was excited. She finally knew that she could be friends with Shella. The excitement on the Visitors face turned to horror when Shella took the magazine and hurled it into the garbage.

"Now get out of my room, you pack rat!" she yelled.

The visitor put on her poker face and gently closed the door. She stood in the dim lit hallway,motionless. Suddenly,she felt a tap on her shoulder and jumped. Monk stood like a shadow grinning.

"Do not worry about Shella, she is always so moody," he said.

The Visitor smiled as she believed that she found an ally. Monk was there to deliver a message.

"I have been looking for you!"

"Really!" the Visitor seemed confused.

"My mom asked me to tell you that you are not allowed to use the phone. You are not allowed to receive or make calls. Is that clear?"

"Clear!"echoed the Visitor.

The Visitor was filled with this unjust oppression. She lived in unfortunate circumstances. In her homeland, the visitor's family was wealthy and did not treat her like this. But now she was thrown into an environment of poverty, mental illness, alcohol abuse, and an atmosphere of obscurity, coupled with neglect.

She dreamed of her fairy godmother rescuing her from such wrath. She wondered if she could escape from such a grave situation. The Visitor bore the verbal abuse patiently, knowing that someday her luck would change and relieve her of this grief.

Julie's vindictive abuse continued. She tried to play the sympathetic victim. Like a spider, she meticulously, spun a web of lies about the Visitor. She created an international platform, where telephonically through gossip, aired her grievances. The very few she befriended listened ardently to the malicious rumors. But they were like the village idiots. They did not have enough intelligence to see that Julie was a loose cannon. The neo cortex of their brains, associated with reasoning, failed to function. Like pathetic insects, they were caught in her web of lies. Some village had lost its idiots. Birds of a feather flock together.

The Visitor was a victim with no hope. Her life had become a tabloid created by Julie. Others soon started to believe Julie. The visitor was ashamed that such malicious rumors were spread. At times she felt like stuffing Julie with candies and beating her up like a piñata. She felt like placing the family in a row and slapping them down like dominos. However, she knew that she could not succumb to such vicious thoughts. She was the better person. She would not resort to violence. One flew over the cuckoo's nest and then there was this Visitor, who flew right into the cuckoo's nest.

"You are the black sheep of the family," spat Dan as Julie crossed his path.

"Kiss my ass," she replied. "And stop grinning like a jackass."

They hurled abuses at each other back and forth like a tennis match. *Love-two,* the visitor thought as though she was keeping score during a match.

Soon all fell into place. It bothered Julie, that all her life in Canada, she lived below the poverty line. It was her own misdemeanors, which placed her in that situation. She was arrested several times for her kleptomaniac tendencies. Wherever she worked she was fired for theft. Her reputation sank like the Titanic. She was unable to get another job, so she collected unemployment. Dan worked as a janitor, all his life until he retired. The visitor did feel pathos for Julie. Julie observed her family living in such wealth, yet she could not achieve success. Her pride caused her to hide her social status and criminal activities, from her nuclear and extended family in Mauritius. Lies rolled out of her mouth like dice. On one particular day the Visitor walked up the basement stairs but stopped with a halt, to eavesdrop on a conversation between Dan and Julie.

"Last night while she was asleep I crept into her room and found her purse," said Julie.

"What did you find?" asked Dan.

"I looked into her purse and removed all the cash she had."

"Good!" exclaimed Dan, "We need cash."

"Then I found her bank book," she whispered.

"Bank book, I want to see that," yelled Dan.

"Shhhhh, she may hear you!"

"What did you find?" asked Dan.

"She has a few thousand dollars in her bank account."

"A few thousand dollars!" he yelled with excitement.

"Yes two thousand."

"We need that money. Call Willy to threaten her. She will hand over the money," plotted Dan, without acknowledging that his voice was so loud. Shella walked in and joined in.

"What are you gossiping about?" she asked.

"Shella go and find our Visitor and tell her that Willy's sons were here last night," said Julie.

"Why?" asked Shella.

"Tell her not to trust Willy's sons because whenever they visit, they always steal money they find."

"You're covering your tracks, you fricken kleptomaniac!" yelled Shella.

They all laughed as if Shella made a witty comment.

"Where is that pack rat?" she asked.

"Reading in the basement," said Dan.

"That's all she does, is read," laughed Shella.

The visitor slid like a snake down a few stairs and resumed reading her book. That's the way she passed her time in such a tarnished household.

CHAPTER 2

It was a beautiful day in October when the Visitor's friend, Michelle, asked her to go to a club. Michelle, a beautiful, blue-eyed blonde was going to meet her boyfriend there. This was the Visitor's chance to escape from the house of horrors, and enter a world of bliss. The Visitor met her kind hearted friend at work. One day after work the Visitor plopped herself on the door step, outside the office. She was so hesitant about going home.

"What's the matter, you look so depressed?"

"Yes, I have to go home to this house of horrors!"

"Well, tell me your story. I have time to listen," said Michelle in a kind and sympathetic tone.

From that day their friendship flourished.

She entered the night club with Michelle and was immediately enthralled by its splendor and beauty. She wore a pair of formal black pants and a rust blazer. Her makeup was done with taste and trend. The dance floor glowed like heaven and the DJ swayed to the beat of his music. Hip-hop, rock, reggae, pop, techno, house music, salsa, and trance rocked the house. It was an exclusive and safe club since the bouncer used his discretion to deny entry to certain folks. It was an upscale nightclub with a strict dress code. The upper class professionals who entered dressed to impress.

The DJ's voice echoed through his powerful PA system. The music bounced off numerous speakers throughout the club. The floor was filled with a smooth mix of music and dancers. The lights were like lightning that throbbed to the beat of the music, flashing in exotic colors. The large, elevated dance floor stretched across almost the full length of the club. The nearby bar was extravagantly lit.

The Visitor was astounded by the elegance of such a luxurious club. The scene was vibrant and she enjoyed each moment, wishing that it would last forever. It was like being transported to a new universe, so different from the dysfunctional household she stepped out of. She was in an urban gem, mingling with the city's nightlife. She was astounded by the elegance of such a luxurious club. It encompassed an extravagant lit up bar. The large open dance floor was elevated and visible from the mezzanine. She had an undisturbed view of the dance floor and the bar. She lounged with Michelle in a cozy seating area just below the dance floor.

The state of the art exotic lights took the night to a more unique level. The live sound of the music bounced off numerous plasmas throughout the club. The inviting dance floor ran almost the full length of the room boasting its fabulous nature. She was transported into a new universe.

They had an undisturbed view and enjoyed each other's company as they talked all night.

"Michelle, what time are you expecting your boyfriend?" she asked.

"He said that he would meet us here at midnight, once he gets off work."

"Are you having fun?"

"Love the place. How about you?"

"It's like I'm at a palace ball. I needed to get away from the madness of that household!"

"I am glad to get you out," Michelle smiled.

It was a relaxing atmosphere, and they sipped their drinks as the night went on. They took every opportunity to dance with young men who politely approached them. They danced to the rhythm of the beat on the crowded dance floor. Everyone had fun indulging in their own exciting and unique dance moves.

"Did you notice the cute guys at the bar?" asked Michelle.

"Ahh, yes I did," she replied.

"Would you like to dance?" asked a man holding his hand out to her.

"Maybe later!" she exclaimed.

As Michelle and the Visitor giggled about the men, the music filled the air with melody, harmony and rhythm. The music was therapeutic for the Visitor. It erased all the problems in her mind.

People spontaneously moved to the rhythm. Customers were able to drink, dance and express themselves by chanting and cheering. The quality of the music was dynamic. At times it was complex and sophisticated.

"There is a group of guys at the table over there. One of them is just staring at you!" Michelle giggled.

"Where?" the Visitor asked.

"To your left," she replied "And he is still checking you out…"

"Oh no!" said the Visitor.

"Oh yes! I've been watching him for a while now. He hasn't taken his eyes off you!"

"Maybe he's looking at you," the Visitor said.

"Oh no no no, he is checking you out!"

The Visitor cautiously looked over her left shoulder. Immediately, she locked eyes with him. A tall, handsome Caucasian man stared at her spellbound. *Could this be love or lust?* she thought. How does his heart choose a partner? She engaged in an inner dialogue with herself.

She knew that at a nightclub most men felt lust—that intense, sexual feeling of physical attraction. That instant chemistry and physical attraction was there as they locked eyes. But she was not looking for true love, so she gave him a teasing grin and turned back to Michelle.

"I am not here to surrender my heart to anyone," she said to Michelle.

"But your spirit is lifted and you're glowing," teased Michelle.

"Stop the sappiness! You're making me blush," she replied.

"Oh my God, what did you do?" asked Michelle. "He's heading in our direction."

"Oh no!" she giggled.

"You are his target!"

The Visitor slyly scanned his movement, as he walked toward her with confidence. She depended on her intuition to tell her if he was just a vulture seeking its prey. She tried to analyze his brain chemistry, and wondered if he was interested in passion and commitment, or just a one-night fling. She felt a strange sense of weakness. He glanced at her and she felt that undeniable spark of sexual chemistry.

It elated his spirit and he felt that obsession of gratification. The object of affection was beside him. He felt that intense desire of affection, coupled with emotional attachment. It was a moment of endearment. She was his object of enthusiasm. His devotion was earnest.

To her, love was not predictable. She felt that most men were jerks, and that most women loved jerks. This was why most good men lost to bad boys. But the Visitor was an intelligent woman. She was not searching for love in all the wrong places. She was always intuitive and the magical sensation she felt could only be generated by Mr. Right. However, she thought with her head and not with her heart, and knew that falling in love meant taking chances. She knew that she had to kiss a lot of frogs before she found her prince. But she didn't want to be single, so she was going to approach this situation carefully. The nightclub was full of players, and he could be one of them.

* * *

He was elated. The object of his desire was near. He was not the type to fall in and out of love. Love to him was an adventure, coupled with hopes and expectations. He appreciated the goodness in others, and lived by ethical standards. He was captivated by good values, beauty, and an engaging personality. He felt intense desire for this beautiful woman, but also knew that he could become emotionally attached to her. His devotion was in earnest.

* * *

The moment was filled with intensity, chemistry, and anticipation.

"Would you like to dance?" he asked as he reached out his hand to her.

"Yes!" she exclaimed.

He kissed the palm of her hand in a gesture of chivalry as he led her to the dance floor. The sweet sound of the Righteous Brothers', "Unchained Melody" filled the air. The words of the song were magical. The hustle and bustle of the nightclub faded into the background as they embraced the dance floor.

Oh, my love
my darling
I've hungered for your touch
a long lonely time.

He gently kissed her cheek as they danced.

Love hit them like a bolt of lightning. They felt like that electric charge could have set the dance floor on fire. Their emotions were strong and instinctive. It felt like turbulence on an airplane. They were weak in the knees and their temperatures rose as their love grew.

Ironically, the words of the song materialized, and that was exactly what God did. God sped their love. It was like the Cinderella fairy tale came true. She was whisked away by her handsome prince. It was magical, phenomenal and extravagant.

After living in the house of horror, with the evil schizophrenic relative and her moody daughter, life changed. She did not have to live with Dan, as each time he spoke verbal diarrhea came out of his mouth. The immigrant visitor had to quickly make a difficult decision. Her first experience in a strange country had been painful. She could not venture out on her own, because of her transitional period of adjustment. She could not continue to jump out of her skin each time Julie tortured her. She had to swallow her pride, and pray that she could get the courage to find a new environment.

After months of unjust oppression, the immigrant visitor received her triumphant reward. Like Cinderella, she lived in unfortunate circumstances that magically ended, and turned into remarkable fortune. She often fantasized about her charming prince, of a different culture, race and nationality. That shining star lit up her life on the dance floor.

God had so graciously bestowed upon her good luck and good karma. God sent down her white chariot, and six months after they met on the dance floor, their fairytale wedding came true. She was transported to an enchanted place that would live on forever. They opened the first dance at their wedding reception to the words of "Unchained Melody."

* * *

After they were married, her Canadian husband sought out a lawyer to discuss the Visitor's immigration status. The lawyer, Mr. Wood, said that they could do an outland sponsorship that would only take a month. But it dragged on for longer. She had to return to Mauritius, to process her spousal sponsorhip. The sponsorship could not be done within Canada. Her lawyer suggested that it would be a faster process, if it was done in her own country.

The words of their song, echoed through her head as she passed through the boarding gates. Tears filled their eyes as she disappeared into the busy terminal.

Unable to bear the loneliness, her Husband flew down to her home country to be reunited. That's when their baby was conceived. The Visitor was five months pregnant when she got an American visitor's visa. She immediately flew to the US to live with friends while she waited for her Canadian immigration status to be resolved. She lived with her Husband's distant relatives in Virginia. Her Husband flew in from Canada on weekends to be with his wife. It was a sacrifice he made each weekend in the name of love.

CHAPTER 3

Despite the cold weather, the Mother experienced hot flashes and night sweats at six o'clock in the morning. She was in bed when she felt a deep excruciating pain that she had never felt before. It began in her lower back and abdomen, and was accompanied by intense cramps. The pain went on and on and made a headache seem mild. It was like she was being hammered by something inside. She did not understand what was happening because her baby was not due until three weeks later. It was so intense, and it was pain that she had not felt before. It was characterized by a deep throbbing action as if she was being hammered by an internal monster. The pain took control over her body, mind, and soul. She couldn't move and couldn't speak. It felt like each organ in her body was going to burst. The excruciating pain erased her memory, impaired her attention span, took away her cognitive thinking and hampered her verbal ability. The sweat flowed from her head like a tsunami heading straight for shore.

She didn't understand what was happening because her baby wasn't due for three weeks. She felt helpless, lonely, anxious, and depressed. The pain was a demon that would not go away, and she didn't know how to cope with it. It was her body warning her that danger was ahead. She couldn't feel her baby move. She wondered if he was going to die inside her.

Her womb began to contract and her uterus tightened. She felt like a python was constricting her body. The pain became stronger and her contractions increased. She spoke to herself,

"Nine months of gain…
Hours of intense pain…
Yet I cannot be vain…
God take me down this birth lane"

She needed a stronger form of pain relief, like some form of anesthetic. The nerves in her body were like a highway with the pain traveling through them like speeding cars. The pain was just erratic. The pain made her feel like the walls around her were closing in.

She mustered up the courage to get out of bed. She was so alone, yet not alone. She carried a baby in her belly, and for his sake she had to be strong and move forward. She felt as heavy as a rock that could not roll. She bravely exited the room and knocked on her friend's door.

"I am in intense pain."

"You are in labor!" exclaimed the friend.

"No, I am not due for three weeks."

"You need to go to the hospital immediately," insisted the friend. "But I need to call your husband first."

"No, don't! He will fly here from Canada on Saturday."

Her friend ignored her and called him. She then rushed the Mother to the nearest hospital.

* * *

Meanwhile in Canada, the Father-to-Be was reacting to the news with great excitement. He called the airport to see if he could purchase a ticket on standby, since it was so early in the morning. To his disappointment, he found out that a nasty snowstorm was interfering with the flights out. An airplane had crashed at a nearby airport because of the snowstorm, so all flights to that airport were postponed. He began to mull over various ways to get to Virginia as quickly as possible.

But the snowstorm did not dampen his spirits. Without hesitation, he got into his car and drove through the stormy weather. It would take sixteen hours to get to Virginia, but he was determined. Nature's most fascinating phenomena could not trap him. He would not panic. Victory, courage, and faith set in and he was determined to be with his wife and baby. He was not going to let the blizzard keep him away from his wife and baby!

The drive to Virginia, from Toronto was exhilarating. He was driving right into nature's fury. The snowstorm was fierce. It faced him like an adversary, holding a white brick wall in front of him. But he courageously faced the storm and drove his little red jeep into harm's way.

Black snow clouds hovered over him. He was ready to face any threat or danger that was ahead. It was like a spiritual race against the evil storm. He compromised his own safety to be with his family. He watched the severe snow storm unfold in front of him. Nevertheless, he was in the pursuit of welcoming his newborn son. He found himself in an unpredictable situation.

Cars and heavy trucks slid off the road. There were many accidents, but he just moved on, in pursuit of welcoming his newborn son. All he could visualize was the birth of his baby. Driving in these conditions was a risk that he had to take.

He was all alone. The radio was his only company. During the trip it was like his only friend. The news and weather updates warned him about the storm he faced.

As he drove, he thought about the day when he had been separated from his wife. She had to leave and go back to her own country because of their immigration lawyer's suggestion. He had to engage in an outland sponsorship, to sponsor her into Canada. Tears streamed down his face, as he realized how difficult parting was. It brought back sad memories.

To add to his somber mood, Mariah Carey's voice filled the car. The song "I Can't Live (If Living is Without You)" played as he remembered his wife's departure.

Being apart from his wife was emotionally painful. But the power of love kept him going. He wiped away the tears and reminded himself that he had to complete this journey to Virginia. His wife was in labor and he had to be there. Nothing could heal his somber spirit. Nothing could reduce the pain of a heartache. He could not pretend. He could not focus on the opposite direction.

He felt a hard lump in his throat that he could not swallow. It felt like a golf ball was stuck in his throat. His heart raced. His muscles were aching. Anxiety was the culprit. The stress, tension, and the anticipation of disaster made the situation worse. It was a sensation that caused his throat to spasm, brought about by stress and anxiety. Stress aggravated the situation. His sense of worry became chronic.

Out of the blue, a tree came crashing down. It crushed the car with an explosive bang. This was followed by a large drift of snow that took away all visibility.

It was a situation that would make anyone stop and panic. But the Father-to-Be had to prevail for the sake of his family. The snowstorm continued to batter him. Death was imminent. How could he survive in such bitter conditions? Death was inescapable and inevitable.

Death, death death…
Multitudes of death…
The Father-to-Be was in the face of death…
The Father-to-Be was in the face of death…
Yes, death, death, death…

Fire engine sirens could be heard in the distance. Danger, disaster, and death filled the air. The angelic whiteness of the snow continued to blanket the region.

CHAPTER 4

The Mother-to-Be continued to pace the corridors of the hospital, experiencing the unending labor pains. Nurses walked by and looked at her with sympathy. However, there was noting that they could do. She continued to pace the long corridors. It was a hall of pain.

She walked back to her private room, hoping to rest despite the deep pain. As she entered the room, her water broke, sending amniotic fluid to the floor. It was like a tsunami rushing with great speed. A nurse rushed in to help. The Mother-to-Be stood in the middle of it all. The baby was coming.

The anesthesiologist rushed in, ready to administer an epidural to eliminate her pain. Not only did the Mother-to-Be have to endure labor pains, but she also had to suffer the excruciating pain of getting the epidural. The anesthesiologist held the large needle in his hand. He then inserted it into her back. He walked the needle tip through the lamina, trying not to puncture the spinal canal. The mother screamed out in pain. She felt the pressure of the syringe and needle on her spine.

"Calm down," said the nurse.

"Ahhhhh! That hurts," yelled the Mother-to-Be.

"It's almost over," assured the doctor as he maneuvered the needle.

"Is my husband here?" she asked with hope.

"Not yet," replied the nurse.

"He is driving here from Canada," said the Mother-to-Be.

"The weather conditions are very bad," warned the nurse.

"I wonder if he is okay," the Mother-to-Be murmured as the epidural kicked in.

The local anesthetic created a feeling of numbness. She could not feel her lower abdomen or legs. The nurse and doctor left the room. As the Mother-to-Be turned, her left leg fell off the bed. But she had no sensation in it. She tried but could not pull it up again. It was numb. She could still feel and use her upper body, so she used the button to call the nurse. The nurse rushed in and helped her place her left leg in position. The Mother-to-Be dozed.

As time ticked by, the epidural wore out, and the pain returned at intervals during her contractions. It was a long day. She wondered about her husband. She had not heard from him.

At two in the afternoon, the baby was ready to enter the world. The mother tried in vain to push him out, but the baby proved to be stubborn. Even with the help of the nurse and doctor, there was no progress. It was like the baby was waiting for his father to arrive.

The baby had his very own agenda. He took control over his own timing. He was now in control. It was his movements that suggested when he was ready. It seemed like he wanted his father to be there. The Mother-to-Be wondered if her husband was alive. Spiritually, birth could foreshadow death. Could her baby's father now be a guardian angel watching them from above?

The hospital room was clean and neat. The walls were a light shade of pink. The curtains complemented the walls, in a darker shade of pink. The floors were made of elegant hardwood and a medium shade of brown. It was almost like a five-star hotel. The room was cozy, warm, and inviting. The attitudes of the nurses and doctors added to the calm and friendly atmosphere. It helped ease the pain felt by the Mother-to-Be. It was a beautiful room that put her into a soothing, good mood, despite the physical pain.

* * *

But what of the Father-to-Be? What was his plight like? He had witnessed a horrible accident. The tree that fell crashed into the car in front of him. He was just yards away, and realized that he could have been that hopeless victim. His journey continued to be challenging.

At 8 p.m., he arrived at a hospital in Virginia, only to discover that he was at the wrong hospital! But he was still excited, knowing that he was close by.

* * *

At 8:30 p.m., the Mother-to-Be's friend arrived to help her. She was surrounded by good company: a friendly nurse, her friend, and the doctor. They waited in for the baby's arrival. At 8:40 p.m. the Father-to-Be walked in to the hospital room with a proud grin on his face. He arrived just in time. And so did his baby boy. Three journeys had come to an end. The Father-to-Be's journey was dangerous. The Mother-to-Be's was a painful one. The baby boy had his own journey as he struggled to enter this world. But now they were all together.

The Father-to-Be had arrived on time to cut the cord, to release the baby who was attached to its mother for almost nine months. The baby boy resembled a telephone receiver, curled up in the doctor's hands. His cry was like a ringtone to his mother's ears.

"Hello, is it me you're looking for?" she joked.

"You may cut the cord," the doctor told the Father.

"Thank you!" he smiled.

"Congratulations!" cheered the doctor.

"Congratulations!" echoed the nurse and the friend.

"My son waited for me!" exclaimed the proud Father.

"Your timing was great," said the Mother with a sign of relief!

The joyful Father followed the nurse as she took the baby out of the room.

CHAPTER 5

At 8:45 p.m. a beautiful, bouncy baby boy entered the world. His first cry was a cry of relief. The jubilant parents embraced the vivacious boy in their arms as they celebrated this euphoric moment as they smiled for photographs.

As the thrilled Father held the baby boy, the obstetrician proceeded to stitch up the Mother who had an episiotomy, which is a surgical incision made through the perineum. The obstetrician took the opportunity to congratulate the parents and confirm when they'd be discharged, as the parents ecstatically echoed in delight, "Thank you!"

The next four days were spent in the home of hospitable relatives. But the anxious young Father longed to return with his baby and wife to his homeland. But his wife had no legal status in Canada. She had been deported on grounds that their marriage was one of convenience.

"Honey, I have an idea. Let's leave early tomorrow morning and drive to Canada. We will tell our relatives that we are visiting friends in New York."

"Oh my God, it's a sixteen-hour trip to Canada," the distraught Mother replied. "How do I cross over the border with no visa or documents? And our baby is just three days old..."

The tormented thought ran through her agitated mind, *Is he suggesting that I abandon my three-day-old baby with our relatives?* she thought to herself.

Nevertheless, the flustered new Father bonded with his wife and baby boy with such passion and tenderness that he teared up at any notion of separation.

Three members of a new family—Father, Mother, and baby—were locked together like players in a rugby scrimmage. It was like they were restarting the game, by entering Canada as a fugitive mother and baby. The interlocked hug brought tears to the new parents' eyes, and they sobbed with tormented panic.

The next morning they stuck to their secret plan. The nervous young Father announced to his baffled hosts that they were taking their four-day-old baby to visit friends in New York. It was a bittersweet moment. They were sad to say good-bye, but they were looking forward to being a family of three in Canada. The hosts expressed their somber goodbyes, bewildered that such young parents chose to travel with a baby in the winter.

"Drive safe and come back soon," the family of three was told as they left.

And the dangerous journey began.

The family of three began their fretful journey from Virginia to Toronto, Canada. It was a journey they had planned yet with no ultimate preparation. They were unprepared, but they had to make the trip. The Father drove his jeep while his wife sat in front with the baby on her lap. The baby boy was silent on his mother's lap, as though he was aware of the seriousness of their journey. If stopped by the authorities, the young couple would be charged with not having the baby in a car seat. But it was a risk they had to take. Escaping to Canada was a chance of a lifetime.

The journey was hard for the Mother. She was still in pain after the labor and delivery. Yet she endured the pain of a sixteen-hour drive.

"I am too nervous to breastfeed our baby in the car," the Mother told the Father.

"Calm down, honey. The hospital gave us a case of formula. But we have no way to warm it up."

Switching a four-day-old from breast milk to formula was a serious decision. But it was the only option in this tense situation. It would be disastrous if the baby rejected the bottle. Not breastfeeding could also be painful for the Mother. Emotions ran high.

Apprehensively, the Mother gently brought the bottle to the infant's mouth. He drank down a quarter of the bottle like a hungry wolf.

"Is he fine with the bottle?" asked the Father.

"He seems to like it," replied the anxious Mother.

The bottled formula was cold, but the baby latched on without a complaint. It was as if he knew that his future was in the hands of his parents and he had to make this work.

The temperature was freezing, with a dominant variety of precipitation. The Father drove through massive amounts of snow. It was below freezing, and the wind and snow created blizzard conditions. What made the journey even more dangerous and difficult were the ten-foot snowdrifts and the snow piles from the plows. It was a dangerous situation, especially while transporting a four day old baby and a recovering mother through such antagonistic winter conditions. But they had to face these risks.

"I am so afraid," said the Mother. "Are you sure we should have left this morning? Deaths occur from hypothermia in these conditions. And there is the possibility of frostbite. And the slippery road conditions could cause accidents."

The mother cried while clutching her new bundle of joy. Her fear was a symbol of her love for and need to protect her newborn.

The Father affectionately caressed his wife's arm and assured her, "I'll drive slowly, honey. It's going to be all right."

The formidable storm affected most of the States with massive power outages. The crippling effects created disaster zones. At one point, their jeep was stuck in the snow.

"We need to get through this storm alive! Oh, my baby! My poor innocent baby boy," cried the Mother. Her mind had moved past fear, and she was determined to protect her child.

"For the sake of our baby, we will get out of this and come out alive," echoed the frantic Father as he tried to hold back his tears.

The strong winds covered the roads in snow. White was the only color visible. It was difficult to drive and maneuver the car through such weather conditions. The snow plows were on the road, but it did not make much of a difference as the snow continued to fall. The snow piles were like mountains lining the streets. Old trees were brought down by the weight of the dense snow.

As large amounts of snow fell it reduced visibility, which made the driving conditions even more difficult. It was a total white out. "Maybe we should turn back," said the Mother.

"The radio said that in some states the roads are clear," replied the Father with a sigh of hope.

"It would have been easier without the baby. We have to think about him. A four-day-old baby will not survive in such conditions," continued the worried mother.

"We will be fine, honey. Don't panic."

The great white monster blanketed the roads in the snow-coated regions of Virginia. The situation was tense and scary as the powerful snowstorm hit the area. To make the situation even more dangerous, the temperature plummeted below zero degrees Fahrenheit. The gusts of wind ravaged through the air as snowdrifts continued to form. Very few cars were on the road as the snowstorm crippled the city. The winter storm covered most of the southeastern parts of the US.

The little red jeep surged its way through the fierce storm. Despite the bad conditions, there were no impassable roads. Huge trucks flew by with such great speed and confidence as they tried to meet their schedules. At times it caused the jeep to sway as huge amounts of snow sprayed the car.

"The driving conditions are getting treacherous. If the weather continues to be this hazardous, we could pull over and wait until it improves. But we have to get across the border tonight," said the Father.

"I don't know what we should do. I'm scared. I can't believe we put ourselves in harm's way," said the Mother.

The psychological pain overtook the physical pain the Mother was feeling. She was sad but could not express her grief. She wanted to be home with her husband and baby, but home was far away. But she had to muster the courage to be strong because she was caring for her newborn baby. He depended on her for strength. Her emotions were like a roller-coaster ride filled with depression, anxiety, and fear. It was a crippling feeling, but she had to remind herself to be strong. She had to stop dwelling on the dangers of their journey. She could not focus on the hopelessness and the danger they faced. Her coping mechanism was hugging the bundle of joy that lay so still on her lap.

The Father was not speeding or driving recklessly, but the jeep began to spin on the icy compacted snow. The father tried desperately to maneuver the car, but it was like a fierce game of ice hockey. The car slid like a ballerina on ice.

"Oh my God, we are going to crash!" yelled the Mother in tears.

"Calm down!"

"Our baby!"

"Oh no!"

The jeep swayed from left to right like a prey being strangled by its predator. The mother held on tight to her baby boy and the door handle. She could not lose her grip because the newborn would fly into the air.

Fear and panic set in. Despite this, the baby brought the parents a sense of inner peace. His situation was now in jeopardy and they knew they had to focus on him. Their lives were in the hands of God. Suddenly, the universe presented an unfriendly situation, of fear and potential danger. Chronic fear weakened the soul and body as The Father clutched the steering wheel and the Mother clutched their baby. The mother could not be selfish because the well being of her newborn depended on her ability to control the situation. She was devoted to her baby boy, which inspired her fear to turn to love. She focused her attention on her baby as the car swayed gracefully like an ice skater gliding with little friction over thin ice.

"Ohhh noo noo!" cried the Mother.

"The car is just sliding. We're fine," said the Father as he tried to control the car.

The car came to a standstill against a barrier of snow. Its tires were stuck in the soft white heap of a snow pile.

"Is the baby fine?" asked the Father with fear and concern.

"I think so," replied the Mother. "I held him close to my chest so that he wouldn't feel the car's movements."

She stared down at the baby who did not seem to be bothered by the drama. All he desired was the warmth of his mother's body.

The Father got out of the car to assess the damage. The temperature was 15 degrees Fahrenheit with winds blowing at 37 miles per hour. These conditions could cause the Father's exposed skin to freeze in thirty seconds.

CHAPTER 6

The situation was terribly dangerous. The baby was wrapped like a burrito in several receiving blankets from the hospital. A thick furry, lime green blanket covered it all like icing on a cake. The Mother's eyes locked intensely on her baby. Her own physical pain had put her in a melancholic state. However, she had to bear the pain and focus her attention on her newborn.

"We have about eleven hours to go before we cross the Canadian border," she yelled out to her husband.

The thought of illegally crossing the border made her feel like she was going to jump out of her skin. Her husband did not hear her and proceeded to push the jeep against the forces of nature.

Suddenly a deep voice in a strong Texas accent asked, "You're havin' trouble, friend? What's the matter?"

The Mother's heart skipped a beat, and she covered the baby with the blanket so that the man wouldn't see the baby's little face.

"I have my wife in the car and we are stuck, sir," explained the Father nervously.

"I'll get the rope from my truck," he said as he returned to the black truck behind the jeep.

The Mother's imagination ran wild as she clutched her baby. Fear gripped her and she became paranoid. At that moment, she thought that the Texan giant could be a serial killer traveling between states.

He could be on a killing spree. In her mind, he fit the characteristics of a serial killer: he was a white male, with an intimidating voice. Images of being tortured or killed filled the Mother's mind like a slide show.

Despite this, she had to be strong for the sake of her newborn and her husband. She put the scary thoughts aside and tried to appear calm.

She felt the car move and heard her husband's overwhelmed voice, "Thank you, sir!" and her overwrought mind settled back to reality.

"Take care and drive safely," the man called out as he left.

"Are you OK, honey? Is the baby fine?" her husband inquired as he fastened his seat belt.

"Yes, eleven hours to go!" There was a sense of relief in the car as she replied.

CHAPTER 7

They stopped at a fast-food restaurant to eat. However, the Mother was in too much physical pain and too nervous to go inside, so they decided to eat in the car. While the car was running, the Father sat in the backseat and the Mother cautiously handed the little boy over to him. The little bundle did not seem to mind, as the Father carefully stripped away the layers of blankets to expose this tiny little newborn.

Within four days, the atmosphere drastically changed from pregnancy to parenting. The Mother looked back at her newborn and thought about those days of anticipating his birth and fantasizing about his arrival. Strong emotions flooded the car as the parents spoke.

"A little human being is now dependent upon us for survival," cried the mother with a lump in her throat. It was a source of excitement as well as a source of stress. They wanted to be the best parents they could be. The transition to becoming parents could be overwhelming. The baby did not come with a manual and taking care of him was a matter of trial and error. But with a sense of confidence the proud father started to change the diaper. Instinct told him that he should gently grasp the baby's ankles and lift him up gently. The baby did not seem to like the lift or the coldness of the wet wipes and gave a cry. The Father noticed that the baby's umbilical stump and circumcision ring were now exposed. He and the Mother knew they had to follow the doctor's instructions in caring for the healing wounds. But the laborious task gave them a sense of pride and accomplishment. Afterward, he fed the baby, and they were ready to continue their arduous journey.

The Mother started to feel tension in her legs. She was afraid this could be the onset of thrombophlebitis, which is an inflammation of the vein and the formation of blood clots. The heavy snow and the whips of cold wind continued, resulting in worse road conditions. The couple was surrounded by darkness. Darkness is metaphorically related to death and can trigger feelings of depression and hopelessness, which the parents were feeling. They drove deeper into the cold, inhospitable darkness. The journey seemed even longer as their spirits dropped.

The Mother looked down at her newborn but she couldn't see him well in the darkness. She could not feel him move, cry, or even breathe. Immediately, the thought of sudden infant death syndrome crossed the Mother's mind. The parents did not want to turn on the dim lights. They were afraid that it would draw attention to the jeep, if the police passed by.

"He is not breathing! Our baby is dead!"

"For God's sake!" yelled the tormented Father.

"Was this trip bad for him?" questioned the worried mother.

She remembered her infant's traumatic birth. She wondered if it had caused any possible injuries to his upper spine or his brain. She recalled reading about genetic risk factors, and wondered if they would cause her baby's death.

"I will pull over at the nearest gas station," said the father in a somber tone.

"I see a gas station sign," replied the mother solemnly.

They wondered if they would have to make the journey to Canada with a lifeless baby. The jeep pulled into the nearest gas station. It was a desolate area with only a few truckers getting a night's rest. The jeep came to a halt and the Father reluctantly turned on the light of the car. They both intensely glanced down at the baby.

"Is he okay, honey?" inquired the Father as he reached out.

"I don't know. He is so still," sobbed the Mother as tears flowed down her cheeks.

Together they removed the first layer of blankets but the baby did not move. The Father picked up the still bundle and began to unwrap more layers. The baby was silent and still. The Mother instinctively placed her pinkie into his mouth. Without any hesitation, the little bundle of joy responded and latched on as if it was a bottle nipple. With great joy, the Father rocked the baby. The Mother took over and fed him with jubilant satisfaction.

CHAPTER 8

They were experiencing such a wide range of feelings. They hated the harsh and bitter winter conditions. Conversely they loved the fact that their baby was well and that they were a loving family.

"I cannot express the joy I feel right now. I am simply ecstatic. Are you tired?" asked the mother in a cheerful mood, despite the conditions. "We have a long way to go. But I am on top of the world knowing that our baby is fine."

"What a strong little boy!" exclaimed the father.

As their snowy journey continued, the weather conditions worsened. Huge trucks passed them by with great haste, as if they were racing for the finish line with a trophy at the end.

Suddenly, out of the blue a huge red truck appeared and honked at them.

"What an impatient driver," yelled the Father.

"Just give him the right of way," replied the Mother.

As the father pulled to the right, the massive trailer sped by like roaring thunder. Speeding like a jaguar into the darkness, the sounds of silence pursued. As the red jeep trudged along, the snow came down harder. The light of the car illuminated the road ahead. The roads were angelic white and glistened.

Suddenly they heard a loud bang that caused the Mother to jump. The Father became more careful in his driving. Ahead of them, a truck had jackknifed, resembling a folding pocket knife. The huge truck carried a trailer behind. It had spun around and was facing the wrong direction. It seemed as though the truck driver had slammed on the brakes, causing the truck to jackknife.

"His speed and the heavy load must have made the situation worse," commented the Father.

"Oh my God!" exclaimed the Mother.

It seemed as if the truck driver slammed on the foot brake causing the truck to jackknife. The trailer and truck covered with compact snow swayed like a prey being killed by its predator and it landed on its side, landing on the curb.

"That was truly the scariest accident that I have ever seen!" cried out the Mother.

"We need to pass him fast in case the truck catches fire," said the Father calmly.

As they drove, they saw other accidents involving jack-knifed eighteen wheelers.

"The need for these drivers to deliver their loads on time causes them to drive in such speed. Obviously these massive ten thousand pound trucks are a part of the nation's economy…Yet look at these traumatic fatalities," lectured the father.

Witnessing this incident made this couple realize that the enormous mass of these trucks made them susceptible to such driving accidents.

"Thank God, we were not hit by one of these trucks!" exclaimed the Mother.

"Their huge size would have severely damaged our vehicle like a flash of lightning," said the Father.

Being trapped by three jackknifed trailers in a blizzard would have been an awful experience. It was almost like a juxtaposition of a child's play room with jackknifed trucks all over the floor.

CHAPTER 9

The strong winds and blowing snow hampered their visibility. The slow-moving storm crawled across the area, and dumped nearly two feet of snow. The parents were gripped with bone-chilling cold. But the couple could not stop to help those truckers in the jackknifed trailers. They had to think of their four-day-old baby. There weren't many other cars on the road, and if the police noticed them, they would wonder about a young baby out in this weather and not in a car seat. The parents were also afraid of the car breaking down in these weather conditions. All they could think of was getting their baby to Canada and to safety. They progressed at snail's pace—surely but carefully.

As the journey progressed Rufus Wainwright's song "He Ain't Heavy, He's My Brother" played on the radio. With tears in her eyes and the baby in her arms, the mother sang along. The lyrics were so meaningful in their situation. It was almost like God provided them with motivation and strength to move on.

As she rocked her baby in her arms, she thought about how the song described what they were going through. It was a long journey to Canada. The words, "That leads us to who knows where" were important to the Mother, because she did not know what her plight would be when she crossed the borders. Most of the other words were the personification of love and concern she felt toward her baby. Despite the fact that she carried him in her arms for hours while still in pain from the delivery, his weight wasn't heavy. She felt like it was almost like the songwriter knew what she was going through. It was her guardian angel encouraging her to be strong.

CHAPTER 10

The music from the radio helped them pass the time. The Mother dozed as the Father kept his eyes peeled on the road. As they drove further north, the weather conditions improved a little. It was amazing how strength and courage kept them moving through such awful weather. They were desperate to be together as a family in Canada, and nobody was going to stop them.

"Wake up, honey, wake up!" whispered the Father.

"Are we there? What time is it?" the Mother asked sleepily.

"It's midnight. We travelled for almost fifteen hours," whispered the Father. "We are going to drive around until after midnight and then cross the Canadian border. The custom officials are more lenient after midnight."

Both parents were fully acquainted with the policies and procedures for entering and exiting the United States. They were familiar with the requirements at the ports of entry. Crossing over meant going through immigration and customs.

The Father was a Canadian citizen so all he needed was his Canadian citizenship documents or his passport.

His wife was deported from Canada because of mean relatives who complained that their status was a marriage of convenience, which was far from the truth. The Mother had entered the US legally from her country of birth. But her American visitor's visa had expired days earlier. The baby was born in the US and was an American citizen. However, his birth certificate was not yet ready and the hospital had promised to mail it to them. Neither the Mother nor the baby could be seen as they crossed the border.

It was a dangerous situation, but love would keep them together. Love was metaphorically their passport to freedom and togetherness. The terrifying weather conditions foreshadowed their dangerous plight at the border. The situation was such a paradox because the mother was married to a Canadian. They married two years before the baby arrived, yet the Canadian immigration system moved at snail pace to process her immigration papers, while keeping them apart. They were determined to conquer their own fears and vanquish the situation to be together. Ironically, the road was long.

Power was in the hands of custom officials who could ruin their lives. The parents knew they could not meet the custom's requirements. They were perpetrating a vicious scenario. They had no illegal goods, but they did have a four-day-old baby with legitimate family ties, but no legal documents. The baby could be taken from them while they endured endless hours of interrogation. They wanted to get past the border without incident. The Father carefully thought out what they were going to do. They did not want to commit a crime, but they had to be together as a family in Canada. The mother was a professional woman; yet in this situation she felt hopeless and melancholic.

The bitter winter wind continued to pierce through every crevice of the car, yet the heat circulated, fighting off the icy weather. The warmth that radiated from the parents also filled the air. But the darkness was still cold and hostile. The surroundings were unfriendly and silent which foreshadowed disaster. Thoughts of being caught crossed their minds. They were heading into dangerous territory, but they had no choice. Anxiety and frustration set in. It was an eerie moment, filled with psychological grief and physical pain. The blanket was over the baby, obscuring his face. The strength of the darkness wreaked havoc on the nervous couple. But it would be the darkness that would help them succeed.

Where was gratitude when they needed it so badly? The blizzard that raged fiercely was now over, but they still stumbled down the long road. The mother maintained her poise, sophistication and dignity while presiding over the situation. It was a mission that they had to accomplish and God was on their side, to preserve their darkest secret. The night was a vengeful one, yet they had to conjure up their plan.

The couple was nervous as their confidence took a leave of abstinence. On a cold winter's day, the father profusely perspired, a trait that vaguely resembled him. They were afraid that their baby could be confiscated and they would suffer endless hours of interrogation if caught. This was a full blown crisis, yet there was no turning back. Their actions had to be quick and decisive because there was no time to ponder over ethical standards.

CHAPTER 11

The ghostly silhouette of the jeep pulled off to the side of the road. The anguished Father glanced at the frantic Mother. They were in utmost despair, placed in such forbidding circumstances.

"Get out of the car," he whispered, conveying a sense of emergency. His heartbeat echoed in the silent night.

"Why? Where are we going?" asked the Mother in a small voice.

The reality of the situation proved to be incomprehensible. They were a privileged family with a good economical status yet in an unprivileged situation. He opened the door for the mother, embracing every moment of this realistic picture. He spread out his strong arms to carry the baby.

"Quick honey! The baby is going to get cold. Take off your winter coat!"

"Why?" asked the mother.

"There is no time for questions," he hurriedly replied.

He moved the front seat forward and ushered her into the backseat. She got into the back and sat on the seat.

"No, honey, sit down on the floor behind the driver's seat and stretch your legs across," he whispered.

"You have to be joking. How can I sit on the floor with my pain," she asked in bewilderment.

But she carefully followed his instructions. He passed the baby to her. She held the little bundle with his legs touching her stomach and his head cradled at her knees. The baby did not seem to mind. He cautiously went along with the plan. He was the personification of innocence. The father covered the mother and the baby with a black bed sheet. He placed his heavy winter coat over the back of the driver seat with the bottom of the coat covering the black bed sheet. On the seat was a green, floral tote bag with essentials for the baby. He put that on the backseat. The mother and baby were on the floor. The mother sat at a 90° angle with her back leaning against the side of the inner car. They were ready to infringe upon the laws of immigration.

Darkness covered the Mother and baby under the sheet. However, the darkness would be their protection. The mother rocked the baby, preparing him for the crossing. Their fate was in the tiny hands of their baby. If he whimpered or cried, they would be caught by immigration officers.

She decided to feed the baby so that he wouldn't cry for milk. She placed the bottle in his mouth. Under the darkness of the sheet, she couldn't see him, but she could hear him latching on. But she couldn't tell if any milk had spilled out of his mouth. As he drank, she heard cars pass by, their breaks grinding in the snow. She predicted that they were heading for the border, yet she did not know how far away it was.

"Honey, the only reason why he would cry again is if his diaper was wet," claimed the father.

"You are right," agreed the mother.

The baby was just four days old, yet they studied his characteristics religiously.

"Here, you change him so he won't cry," the Mother said as she handed the Father the baby from under the sheet.

He changed the baby while explaining the situation to him.

"You have to be quiet, baby. We need to make this trip."

The baby made strange gurgling noises as though agreeing with every word of his father.

"Sleep tight and don't cry," he lovingly whispered to the little bundle, and handed him over to the Mother who hid back under the sheet. She rocked him on her knee, preparing him for the journey ahead. The Father drove around to prepare the mother and child for the traumatic experience ahead.

CHAPTER 12

The Father had crossed the US-Canada border several times, so he was aware of what he was doing. His border crossings always went smoothly. Now, he had his passport documents in hand. He turned off his radio to prepare himself for the booth. He had to forget about his wife and son at the back and portray a façade of confidence. His composure had to be sincere and polished. He knew that border officials would question the bag at the back.

"Honey, just be quiet and I will tell you when it is all over. Try your best to keep the baby quiet," he calmly stated.

"Okay," she whispered.

"I love you, honey, no matter what happens," he whispered.

"I love you, too. Good Luck."

Eerie silence filled the air. It was like she was trapped in a black hole with her baby. She was transported into her own world of orbiting distant stars. She thought about her father, who had tragically passed away several years ago. She wondered if he was her guardian angel, and hoped that he was there to protect her in this crucial moment.

She imagined her father in a plane of existence determined by God. She wanted to be transported to his dimension in an infinite universe beyond, where she did not require a passport to freely travel from place to place. She would live in a world of freedom. She appealed to God to safely transport her and her baby to Canada, a land of opportunity and freedom.

She had always experienced good karma for her good deeds. She sowed her good seeds and waited to reap the benefits. She called upon any entity to guide her through this difficult path. Images of her father continued to cross her mind, strengthening her mind and body. She focused on her baby, sleeping peacefully through such a terrible ordeal. Thoughts of tremendous persecution, suffering, imprisonment, and interrogation were eliminated from her mind. She was in a realm of darkness, her body was paralyzed with fear, but she was still filled with positive energy and bold hope. This would be a life-changing experience.

CHAPTER 13

In the death of silence, a strong, bold voice cut through the silence like dynamite exploding. His voice was strong enough to command a battalion of soldiers. The Mother was afraid that it would disturb the baby, so she put her pinkie close to his mouth. It would pacify him if he cried. This little baby held the key to their future. Their lives were in his powerful little hands. Suddenly, he was the symbol of freedom. This jumbo shrimp, so big and powerful, yet so tiny. If he cried, whimpered or made the slightest sound they would be arrested, crossing the border illegally.

The moment was so tense and all three—the Mother, Father and baby—had to play their parts well. One wrong move and it would be the end. This situation personified death. It was so risky yet so necessary. The mother and baby were crashed into a confined space on the floor of the back seat. If caught they risked imprisonment, as they illegally embarked on their journey to freedom. It was not political or economical freedom, but the freedom to be together as a nuclear family unit.

As the border official looked through papers, the Mother silently thought about the Fourteenth amendment of the United Stated of America.

"All persons born or naturalized in the United States and subject to the jurisdiction thereof are citizens of the United States of America." Her baby was born in the US, so he was an American. But he was not their anchor to claim residency. She was still an illegal alien, who did not qualify for amnesty. So she couldn't stay in America and she wouldn't be allowed in Canada.

She imagined being in the courtroom where the prosecutors would bring tough criminal charges against them. They would have to face the federal officials. She knew that the immigration violations fell under the civil statues. She understood the magnitude of such indictments. They would be subjected to pleading guilty and sentenced for a crime. But is it a crime to desperately want to stay together as a family of three? The mother wondered why something so wrong felt so right. Both parents were no harm to the US and did not have a propensity to commit any other crimes.

She felt the warmth of the baby on her legs. She was stiff and numb yet could not move. The slightest movement would upset the baby. The darkness beneath the black sheet provided the mother and baby with some warmth and security.

Once again the booming voice of the immigration official rang through the air. The Mother felt so guilty because her poor husband was left alone to answer all the questions while staying calm. Even though he had proper Canadian documentation and needed no additional screening, she knew his heart carried a heavy burden since he was transporting illegal cargo.

"How long have you been in the United States, sir?" he asked.

"Just five days," said the Father.

"Did you purchase any goods?" His voice rumbled like an earthquake with a 7.5 magnitude.

"No, just visiting friends, sir," replied the Father shaking like he experienced the aftermath of an earthquake.

"Any goods in your trunk, sir?"

"I have no trunk, sir" the Father replied.

"That will be ___ dollars," he said.

"Here you go, sir," the Father said as he handed him the exit fees.

"You may proceed."

"Thank you, sir" the Father said with a sigh of relief and drove on.

The red jeep was a convertible. It had a soft, white plastic covering with vinyl plastic windows and a white leather exterior cover. With the wild, windy conditions the top was covered in slush. It was hard to see through the windows. The front seats were visible through the glass windows, though the back seats were not, so the jeep looked more like a two-seater.

The Father maintained his calm composure as he drove away from the US border. He heaved a sigh of relief, knowing that he had successfully passed one border.

"We just left the US border," he whispered to the Mother.

"Be quiet! Shhhh!" she replied agitatedly.

"We will arrive at the Canadian border soon," he calmly explained.

"Do not talk to me!" she nervously whispered.

She felt as if she was in a room full of loud speakers and microphones. Every word and movement would be amplified, announcing their presence to the border officials. In a state of paranoia, she chose to take a vow of silence. Also, talking could wake up the baby. They had to keep him quiet.

However, with sounds of silence came emotions and memories that placed a burden on the Mother's frame mind. She thought about childbirth and what she had been through to bring this beautiful baby boy into this world.

Ironically, they were forced to adopt a vow of silence in such a serious situation. However, if they were caught by the Canadian border officials, they would have the right to remain silent, as a legal procedure while undergoing a police interrogation. They will have the right to silence.

The mother freed herself from the onslaught of negative thoughts and legal thought patterns. She reached out to her inner silence in order to address the divine spiritual powers. In the Hindu scriptures it was an act of spiritual growth associated with meditation and respect for God. She wanted spiritual enlightenment in such a tense moment.

She chanted a silent prayer for a safe journey to Canada. The silent prayer brought her in touch with the great universal power, and she prayed that her baby would remain silent. The silent prayer sealed her eyes and mouth yet opened up her heart, which was filled with requests to the supreme power to keep them safe.

Chapter 13

She was a fugitive seeking refuge in the love of her family. She was "on the lam," which was slang for being on the run from the law. She thought about political leaders who were once fugitives but were later deemed heroes. Unlike them, however, she was in search of a safe haven for her husband, baby, and herself. The safe haven was Canada.

CHAPTER 14

The Father held the steering wheel firmly, and made sure his right foot gently pressed on the accelerator. Fear took control of him. His fear and anxiety over dealing with the Canadian border officials made him almost motionless. But his heart beat violently and such palpitation sped up with a greater sense of fear. Despite the cold, perspiration dotted his face like beads of water. The hairs on his skin stood erect like soldiers waiting for commands from their captain. A shiver ran through his muscles. His mouth dried up.

He glanced at himself in the rear-view mirror and was horrified to see a grimace on his face. His eyes were wide, his pupils dilated. His face was scarlet red and wet as if he had been in a torrential rain. He resembled a very nervous Frankenstein. He was afraid that his appearance would alert the Canadian immigration official. The Father looked fear in the eye and realized that he had a choice of fight or flight. He chose fight because he had to regain his calm composure for his family. He had to suppress the fear to conquer the situation.

He slowly approached the Canadian border. He made sure he had his Canadian citizenship card ready. He was prepared to answer any questions directly and politely to avoid causing any suspicions. The border was quiet, as he had predicted.

The Canadian immigration officer spoke with a polite and calm voice. His voice was like a gentle tune from a radio station. The Mother did not think that such a sweet voice would intimidate her baby and make him cry.

"Where are you from?" the official inquired.

"I am Canadian, sir," the Father replied.

Although he appeared to be calm, the Mother sensed that there was a crack in his voice. Hopefully, she was the only one who could recognize that he was nervous.

"How long have you been away?"

"Just five days, sir," he replied.

"What was the purpose of your trip?"

"Visiting frie-friends, sir," the Father stuttered.

"Are you bringing anything with you that you want to declare?"

"No, sir."

"What is in that package on your backseat?"

Oh my God, thought the Mother. *This Canadian immigration official was sharp enough to predict that her husband was carrying illegal cargo!*

Tears streamed down her face as she stroked her baby's face. She imagined the official opening the door and uncovering them as though he was unveiling the statue of Madonna and her child. She sat still underneath the black bed sheet. Her heart was in her mouth.

Her baby seemed to hold his vow of silence. She knew that when the car door opened, her baby would be alarmed by the cold weather and give out a loud cry.

CHAPTER 15

The Mother was immersed in fear. With the manifestation of fear she felt the urgent need to visit a washroom. She felt like her body was losing all strength. This was a psychological phenomenon. She had never experienced such fear before. But she did not lose her grip on her baby boy. She held him with a firm yet gentle touch. His head lay on her knee and he slept like an angel.

Fear bulldozed her thoughts and she could not perceive the danger ahead. In the face of the officer she knew that she had to give in to submission, compliance and acquiescence. This fear inspiring force was too powerful to beat. She was budged into giving in and the sense of demoralization overtook her mind and body. Once again the polite voice of the official echoed through the air.

"What is in the package on your backseat, sir?"

Panic set in as fast as lightning. It was an unwelcomed emotion that approached like a wild animal hastily darting across a road. It occurred at the wrong time to put an end to all thought and block out all form of logical reasoning. Panic was accompanied with intense anxiety and agitation. The anxiety threatened to stop them from thinking logically. Both parents felt the panic. However, the baby still remained calm. The Mother worried that there could be a chain reaction. The baby would feel their stress and cry out.

Fear, worry and anxiety accompanied with stress flooded the atmosphere of the car. The preventative measures could not be reached in such a critical situation. The mother's psychological and physiological frame of mind changed with a matter of seconds. Amid the fear and worry, the voice of the immigration official, echoed through the air several times.

"What is in the package on your backseat, sir?"
"What is in the package on your backseat, sir?"
"What is in the package on your backseat, sir?"
"What is in the package on your backseat, sir?"

These words echoed through the silent night. The mechanical vibrations of his voice travelled through the air. It was an eerie phenomenon with the speed of sound reaching the U.S. border, returning with explicit magnitude.

The echo of his voice reflected off the hard, red surface of the jeep and the border fence. These were words that rung continuously in the mother's mind.

The intensity of her anxiety increased. She experienced the pain, stiffness, tension, pressure and spasm through her back that was against the car. Her body spasmed with pain and tension. Her body temperature increased. She could feel her skin burning with itchy and prickly sensations, followed by numbness. Her chest tightened and a sense of dizziness took over. The words echoed in her mind.

We are caught. We are caught. We are caught. Oh my God! We are caught.

She could feel her heart palpitations. Her heart raced like a horse running for the finish line. Her muscles began to twitch. She felt lethargic with an urge to urinate. The car floor seemed to be moving under her, as her rib cage tightened. She was afraid she was having a heart attack, as her emotions ran high. She could sense impending doom.

However, she reminded herself that she could not be irrational when she had her newborn on her lap. She had to eliminate all the horrible thoughts and feelings. Her precious little cargo depended on her for survival. She could not behave like a hypochondriac or indulge in a premature death.

The Mother was no fool. She was fully aware of the implications of an anxiety attack. For the sake of the newborn baby, she had to maintain her calm composure.

The baby thrust his legs out, which worried the mother. She had to comfort him to keep him still and quiet. She knew that this could mean that he was waking up. This was not the time for even a gurgle. The slightest noise would alert the immigration officer. This was not the situation for the baby to crave any meaningful attention, or be upset by this experience. He slept a lot during this long journey and maintained his calm composure. The mother paid attention to all of his signals. She was most alarmed when he thrust his leg out because she knew that this could mean that he was waking up. This was not the time for any vigorous, intense or spontaneous cry or even a gurgle.

The Mother was armed with her pinkie, to respond to any form of distress. She stuck out her pinkie like the Queen of England holding a small cup of tea. In the darkness, she could not see if he puckered up his lips with the intent to cry. But she had to be prepared for any spontaneous situation.

She heard a whimper and immediately maintained physical contact. He quieted, and it was almost like this little baby boy comprehended their plight and chose to protect his parents. Yet the words still echoed in the mother's mind.

What is in the package on the backseat, sir? What is in the package on the backseat, sir...sir...sir...sir?

The voice of the immigration officer still filled her head, like a hallucination. It was not a case of being paranoid or schizophrenic but it was the fear of being in such a malicious situation. She could visualize the consensus of reality and that was being sent to prison for illegally crossing the border, with a new born baby.

CHAPTER 16

The Father heard his own voice and knew that it sounded like he was giving a speech or reciting an oral presentation. The words came out with such nervousness. He knew that part of the nervousness came from his feelings of guilt over the illegal thing they were doing. His hands shook and his voice cracked. His heart beat faster. These were symptoms that he could not avoid. Ironically, he was intimidated by the calm voice of the immigration officer.

He could not move away from the parameters of the questions. He had no cue cards or prompters to take away his nervousness. It was a moment of panic. The father thought about how he felt when he watched his child being born, and realized that was a different form of nervousness. Watching his baby boy burst out of the womb, like a cannon being released made him jump out of his skin. However, that nervousness soon turned to excitement and joy, as he glanced down at a baby that resembled him.

The words of the immigration official also echoed through his mind. He knew that he had to answer that question believably, in order to prevent any suspicion from forming.

Meanwhile, that green, floral print bag sat on the backseat like a mystical package. Its content could get the parents into serious trouble. If opened, it would reveal baby pajamas, newborn hats, booties, scratch mittens, a bunting bag, bibs, cotton blankets, burp cloths, a breast pump, changing pad, baby ointment and lotion, wet wipes, hooded towels, and other baby necessities. The immigration or customs official would be suspicious of a single man traveling with these items.

The mystery bag sat on the seat above the mother and baby with an element of suspense. The gritty realism of the bag would be the logical solution for the customs official to expose the plot and solve the crime. To the parents, it was a weird menace that could expose their situation. It was a symbol of emotional disaster. Like a roller coaster ride, the floral bag created nervousness and anxiety in both parents. It was like a suspense thriller that had twists to the plot. The contents of the bag determined the family's fate. The bag would be the singular item responsible for the arrest of the parents. It was the symbol of ultimate destruction. It was the clue to expose the mystery. It contained the secret of that would expose everything.

The Father finally answered the official.

"Oh…just…just personal belongings." This time his voice was more nervous than before.

"Any alcohol or cigarettes?"

"No, sir!"

The Canadian immigration officer handed the Father his citizenship card and gestured for him to proceed.

"Thank you!" exclaimed the Father and drove off into the still night.

Kass Ghayoure

CHAPTER 17

The moon shone down upon the red jeep as it drove off. It lit up the dark sky, looking over the couple with a smile on its bright face. Under the spot light of the moon, the red jeep progressed on. The spotlight of the moon followed the jeep as if following a celebrity. The powerful beam of light followed the vehicle, as though it could prevent it from any night attacks.

The moon was like a spiritual angel that protected and guided this family of three to freedom. Its wings spread over them like a blanket of protection. It was like a heavenly host welcoming the fugitive mother and her baby into Canada. It exemplified the parallels between light and darkness. It paced itself on a systematic hierarchy leading the family through the mystical darkness. In all glory the red jeep drove away from the Canadian border, as if it was moved by the motion of the moon, and angelic circle above. It posed as a messenger of God with an appropriate mission to lead the family to safety. The moon was like a bodyguard, protecting the fugitive mother and baby, removing all their restrictions and providing them with safe passage. It transported the Mother and baby to freedom.

"WELCOME TO CANADA, HONEY!" yelled the Father with tears of joy.

"Just keep driving! What's wrong with you? I will talk to you when we get home," whispered the Mother still filled with fear.

"It's all over, honey, we just passed the Canadian border," he said.

"Really?"

"Yes!"

"Oh my God, we need to sell this story to a movie producer!"

She hugged her baby with passion and satisfaction. The journey of fear was now over, though they still had to reach their cozy home in Toronto.

CHAPTER 18

The parents' journey did not end there. They had to drive for another two hours from the Niagara border to their home in Toronto. However, this was a different journey. The stress of crossing the border took a toll on them and they were exhausted. Nevertheless, the four-day-old baby boy went along without fussing.

"What are you doing?" asked the Mother.

"Just pulling over at this shopping plaza," replied the Father.

"It's fine. I will wait until we get home," said the Mother.

"We have another two hours to go. Besides, you're safe now. We are in Canada, so there is nothing to fear," said the Father with a sigh of relief.

He pulled over and opened the door to let the mother and baby out. She plopped herself on the front seat with such relief that part of it was all over.

The extreme terror had now subsided. They were happy to be together to celebrate freedom. Anxiety, panic, and fear had all vanished into the dark night.

* * *

It was about 1:30 a.m. and the couple was driven by contentment, love, satisfaction, and the joy of beginning their new life together. Their happiness could not be measured. These positive feelings provided them with the strength they needed to move on as a married couple and a family.

"I cannot explain this emotion that I feel right now," said the Father.

"That makes two of us," replied the Mother.

"He was such a good boy. Not a cry or a whimper throughout the trip," the Father murmured, stroking the soft, red cheeks of his newborn.

"This is a lucky miracle. Oh, my baby boy, you made it all happen!" rejoiced the Mother.

"Are you hungry?" asked the Father.

"No I am in a state of nostalgia. I'm too happy to be hungry. All I need is my own cozy bed. Let's keep going," she replied with a broad smile.

As their journey progressed, the night was still and the roads were clear. The Mother could actually appreciate the aesthetic beauty of the night. Happiness spread through her entire body like a virus. She held the bottle of milk close to the baby and he drank quickly, as though he felt the same sense of relief.

Her stress had vanished into the night, and she was able to connect with her baby. With a better sense of self-actualization and satisfaction, she was able to regain her self-esteem, knowing that all her attention could be directed toward her baby.

She received the ultimate freedom from psychological suffering. Her compassion for her baby was the ultimate source of happiness.

* * *

The Father felt the same intoxicating happiness. Being with his wife and newborn strengthened him in mind and spirit. He wanted to seize this happiness and treasure it forever.

"After a day of relaxation, we will take the baby to the birth and registration department to get him his Canadian citizenship," explained the Father.

"Will that be a problem?"

"No, I am a Canadian and he is my son," he replied.

"Well, I guess we will have to go back to the same lawyer, Mr. Wood, to process my immigration papers once again," she commented.

"He should have suggested an inland sponsorship in the first place. Instead, he forced you to return to your country to do an outland sponsorship. He has done nothing for us, but drained us of several thousands of dollars, "replied the Father.

The entire problem began when they consulted a top notch lawyer called Mr. Wood. The couple was married in Canada. They could have engaged in an inland sponsorship based on humanitarian and compassionate grounds.

However, the lawyer suggested that the spousal relationship did not constitute sufficient grounds for an inland sponsorship, and asked the wife to leave the country, in order for him to process an outland sponsorship. The lawyer promised that this would take up to three to six months after the application was submitted. The false information provided by him resulted in their dilemma. One year had passed by, and the couple were still not reunited in Canada. The father travelled across the ocean to join his wife in her home country.

This is when the baby boy was conceived and the rest was history. This is when the mother applied to legally travel to U.S.A with an American visitors visa when she was five months pregnant. The father left his business in Canada to drive down to see her, as she lived with his close family friends. The end product was when the baby was born in U.S.A which made them an instant, happy family.

* * *

The journey through the streets of Canada from Niagara to Toronto was so peaceful. The road conditions were so clear with so much of visibility. The street lights and lamp posts lined the streets shedding light on the clear roads. The light served the purpose of providing for security. The incandescent lamps shone upon the little red jeep and the sweet face of the baby was then visible. The atmosphere was so calm and jovial, as opposed to the previous hours of intense fear. Even the radio played songs as if it was also celebrating the family's victory. The lyrics of Paul Simon's "Homeward Bound" echoed through the car.

The moon had faded, as if to imply that they were now safe. The sun rose and the morning was quiet. Yes, they were homeward bound. All their emotional and psychological chains were removed and they were set free. All their thoughts were focused on the comfort of being back home. Their long journey was drawing to an end.

"He just finished all his milk," said the Mother.

"It is almost like he felt the same sense of relief that it's all over," replied the Father.

The baby's tiny eyes looked up at his mother with a sense of satisfaction. The mother carefully lifted him up to her shoulders and gently stroked his back. The baby gave a loud burp accompanied by a sigh of relief.

A police cruiser passed by and made eye contact with the couple. Shortly after, the Father looked at his rearview mirror and noticed that the police cruiser turned around and was headed in their direction.

"Put down the baby!" exclaimed the Father. "I think he saw you carrying the baby in the front seat. We do not have a car seat and that means trouble."

"Yes, the baby is down and out of sight," whispered the nervous mother.

The police cruiser pulled next to the little jeep, on the Mother's side. He looked into the car. The Mother and Father glanced at him and smiled. He was on his beat. There were no visible visual or audible warnings. He was just monitoring the area. The mother and father were tense as they exchanged glances. He gave them that confused look as if to say, "Did I notice a baby in the front seat?"

The markings on his cruiser brightened up the morning and added more visibility to the road. His flashing light and rotating beacons illuminated the car. He didn't use his siren, which could have alarmed the baby. The Mother locked eyes with the officer. He nodded his head, and smoothly took off into the morning mist.

"That was a close one!" exclaimed the Mother.

"He must have thought he saw you holding the baby," sighed the father.

"Ummm, just checking", she calmly expressed.

Once again they were homeward bound as they drove into the misty morning. Safe! Safe! Safe!

CHAPTER 19

Finally, their journey came to a pleasant end as they pulled up to their home sweet home. The mother got out of the car and walked to the door. After sitting for almost twenty hours with the warmth of the baby on her lap, it was almost like she forgot how to walk. The Father was exhausted after driving for many hours. As they opened the door to their warm and cozy nest. It was such a friendly and welcoming atmosphere. There was no fear or anxiety. *There's no place like home,* they both thought to themselves. The air was friendly as they embraced the comfort of home in Toronto, Canada.

They tried to get the sleep that was well deserved; however the personality of the baby began to take a toll over the situation.

"It is so good to be home," whispered the Mother.

"I am still in shock that it is all over. It was a total nightmare," said the Father.

"We will have a wonderful story to tell him when he grows up," said the Mother with tears of joy.

They tried to get some well-deserved sleep, but the baby cried out to get his parents' attention. Their parental instincts kicked in and the Mother tried to interpret his wails, groans, and moans.

"He is not hungry because I fed him," she said.

The Father picked him up with no hesitation, and rocked him with the baby's face close to his chest.

"I carried him for twenty hours and he felt the warmth of my body. He expects to be carried. That's why he is crying," realized the Mother.

"I don't think that he likes my skinny chest," replied the Father as he handed the baby to her.

The baby instantly calmed down. Home was a new experience for him. He was sensitive to the lights, the noise of the heating unit, and the other sounds of the new surroundings. It was being carried that reassured him—it was his way to blow off steam.

"Can you imagine if he was cranky when we crossed the border or on the trip?" exclaimed the Father.

"His temperament and personality is taking shape," said the mother.

With several failed attempts, she tried to place the pacifier in his mouth but he spat it out furiously as if to say, "What nonsense is this? If it does not produce milk, then why do I need such a device in my mouth?"

He did not want the pacifier because it did not resemble the mother's breast.

The parents acted quickly, and the very next day they applied for the baby's Canadian citizenship. There were no problems, and the whole process went smoothly.

CHAPTER 20

After a week's leave of absence, the father decided to return to his business in Toronto. He and the Mother decided to take the little baby boy to introduce him to his manager and employees.

They entered through the back door and the father's manager immediately spotted the family. His first reaction was one of instant shock. He went as pale as a frozen snowman. He shook like a leaf as the Mother handed him the baby. The initial shock turned into joy. He looked down at the baby in disbelief.

"How did you get into Canada with the baby?" he asked.

"Well, the baby will tell you that when he grows up," joked the Father.

"Oh, what delightful news...a cute baby boy!" he exclaimed.

"Congratulations!" yelled the other employees.

Happiness warmed the atmosphere. It left everyone breathless. Everyone rejoiced, seeing the newborn and the brave parents. It was a celebration of life and freedom. All faith was in this little baby boy, and the parents did not want to dwell on the awful things that they had to endure. That entire journey was a total oxymoron of joy mingled with fear.

The joy of celebrating the birth of the baby boy and the fear of being caught during their journey, were like two sides of the same coin. Who knew that joy and fear could go hand in hand?

Joyful employees and a shocked manager surrounded the family of three. This was the celebration of the extremes of life, with a sudden "high", influenced by the appearance of the newborn. The enhanced feeling of joy filled the place. However, the manager still trembled with shock. He trembled like an earthquake, with a 5.5 magnitude.

The parents joined in the celebration. They had overcome the struggle of a major obstacle. The hardship did not register on their faces. They celebrated life as a great adventure, and were ready to move on with positive energy, in order to lead fulfilling lives. Laughter filed the room. It was a priority of emotional health, as opposed to the fear they felt days before. They discovered joy in the saddest moment. This made them strong enough to adopt a positive outlook on life.

CHAPTER 21

A few days later they decided to address the Mother's immigration status. The family of three visited the office of their lawyer, Mr. Wood. The mother was not happy with this lawyer because he had cost them thousands of dollars, yet did nothing to improve her immigration status in Canada. He had a reputation of being a top-notch lawyer; however, he had so far done nothing to live up to his reputation.

The Mother concluded that this lawyer knew how to manipulate a situation in order to milk his clients for thousands of dollars. It was that money that made him a millionaire and earned him respect from the community. It was his wealth that earned him the reputation of being a top lawyer.

All he did for the couple was send letters to the immigration officials. Both parents were fluent in English and they could have represented themselves. But the immigration system prompted them to seek legal assistance. The parents decided to try again, and give him one more chance.

With the baby in tow, they walked into his office. It was luxurious—it had exquisite antique furniture and royal Persian rugs. It was almost like they were visiting some imperial power, to see its royal residence. It was a beautiful office, with its spacious size and elegant atmosphere. It was a place that no human tongue or even words could describe. The elegant furniture stood in the appropriate corner. The executive secretary was stationed behind her imported reception desk.

"Do you have an appointment?" she inquired in a bourgeois tone, revealing her social class status, in a bourgeoisie office.

"Yes, we are here to see Mr. Wood," replied the Father.

"What is the case?" she asked.

"He knows," replied the Father.

She confirmed their names and told the Mother and Father to sit down. They sat themselves on a luxurious couch. The Father proudly cradled his newborn in his arms.

"Beautiful place," said the Father.

"Yes, very bourgeois," said the Mother in a sarcastic tone.

"Yes, the wealthy members of the Third Estate. "replied the Father.

"The ruling class, that controls all means of coercion… functioning capitalist, that did nothing to help us," continued the Mother. "Such materialism surrounds us… and the hypocrisy of the aristocratic lifestyle… living on our dollars and yet doing nothing to help us. That is shameful." The mother was angry because the whole process cost so much.

"That's what we have to face, dealing with these top lawyers," he calmly stated.

The secretary looked up, with her reading glasses perched at the tip of her nose. She had a deep frown on her face, making her look like a chubby pooch. She eavesdropped on the private conversation of the parents. Nevertheless, the ringing of the phone took her back to her busy schedule.

The parents continued to look around, admiring the expensive Persian rugs that lined the dark mahogany hardwood floors. It resembled the elegant, distinguished style of the Persian culture. The hand-woven carpets, which probably cost millions, resembled the shining jewel on the floor. The details of the rug were very intricate, with fibers in exotic colors. The Father lifted the corner of one huge rug and confirmed its authenticity. It was obviously handcrafted and was not machine made.

It reflected on its arduous process of traditional handmade masterpiece, fit for a king. Those Persian rugs served as a symbol of sophistication with its laborious threading and intricate pattern. It was a testament to their legacy. The artifacts around the room revealed the cultural interest of the collector. They were definitely the most prized possessions of an ardent traveler. It revealed its aesthetic beauty and artistic creation. Its function evoked the sense of sight, as it depicted an artistic era. They were pieces that curators would collect at a museum.

Even the paintings on the wall of the law office had distinct physical qualities that could be identified as a masterpiece. It could be complimented for its artistic merits, and economic value.

The parents' admiration for the artifacts were interrupted by the secretary who informed them that the lawyer would not be too long.

"He is just finishing with a client," she informed them.

"Thank you," the Mother replied.

"The wait seems to be longer than our journey from Virginia to Toronto," joked the Father.

"With the same anticipation," said the Mother.

The lawyer soon appeared dressed in his three-piece suit. His wavy gray hair was brushed back, revealing his chubby and friendly face.

"Well, hello there," he spoke with a deep, loud voice.

"Hello!" echoed the Mother and the Father in chorus.

"What are you doing here in Canada?" he addressed his question to the Mother in confusion. And then continued as though they were special guests, "Please come into my office."

They sat down in his office and yet Mr. Wood was not in a state of shock to see the mother and the baby. Though he was initially confused, Mr. Wood seemed more amused to see the Mother and the baby. He called his daughter and son-in-law into the room. They were also lawyers and partners in his law firm. He wanted them to share this unique experience with him. From the legal standpoint they could have been just witnesses.

Mr. Wood's daughter was not as friendly. She dressed like a man in brown pinstriped pants and a man's buttoned-down white shirt with green pinstripes. She walked like a man and spoke like one, too. She was a typical bourgeoisie, with an arrogant attitude. She stared at the family, trying to read their minds.

"How did you enter Canada?" asked Mr. Wood with a friendly smile.

"Through the US-Canadian border," replied the Mother.

"Were there any problems?" he continued, fascinated.

"No, none," replied the Mother.

"Where was the baby born?"

"In Virginia," replied the proud Father, still cradling the baby in his arms.

"So where do we go from here, now that I am back in the country?" inquired the Mother.

"Well, since we're starting over, it is a new case. I am going to give this case to my daughter," he replied with a jovial smile.

The daughter straightened herself up, as she sat tall in her executive chair. She still had an unfriendly look on her face. She stuck out her long arms to shake the hands of both parents.

What game is this man trying to play with us? thought the Mother.

"But you have our immigration spousal application and it is still the same case," commented the Father, getting irritated.

"The first step would be for us to call the Canadian police and notify them about your entry," he said.

"They will come to the office and arrest you," said the arrogant daughter.

"From there, we will process another file to release you and fight the case," replied Mr. Wood with the same relaxed smile on his face.

The Mother was no fool. She could smell a rat. She knew exactly what Mr. Wood and his daughter were up to. They wanted to start another case so that they could charge more money. She knew that this case could exceed fifty thousand dollars, if dragged on in court. Once again, Mr. Wood would be the victor, pocketing the money.

Through her past experiences with him, she realized he enjoyed dragging a case along in order to obtain more money from such a deal. Each phone call to him cost money. Each appointment was $120 an hour.

On no occasion did he present himself at any immigration hearing or appointment. He just sat in his cozy, luxurious, bourgeois office and got his secretary to type letters which he sent to immigration.

He did not make this immigration process efficient or pleasant. In this time of crisis and difficulty, he was only prepared to add fuel to the fire. The parents thought that utilizing the experience of a lawyer to press their case would speed up the process, but they were wrong.

The words, *"We will call in the police and have you arrested!"*

"We will call in the police and have you arrested!"

"We will call in the police and have you arrested!"

echoed through the minds of the parents several times. They could not believe that it was happening all over again. She was not an illegal alien; she was married to a Canadian, which by law qualifies her for immigration status in Canada. She was not remaining beyond the authorized period of legal entry. This immigration case did not depend on the motion of the prosecutor.

"We will contact you again after we discuss the issue," said the Father, hastily exiting with his family.

The couple never returned. They could not trust him with their case because he had the wrong intentions. He just wanted their money.

After another week of relaxation at home, the parents decided to reapply at the immigration offices.

They took matters into their own hands and reapplied for the Mother's immigration status in Canada. They did not need a lawyer. They were fully able to articulate their own problems to the immigration officers.

Confidence in gaining self control possessed them. All positive thoughts filled the minds of the parents. They maintained a positive demeanor to make success in their situation more probable. Power visited them to which added success to their relationship, financial situations, business, health, and joy of being together. Changing her immigration status was smooth sailing. It did not require any police intervention or arrest. The Mother became a Canadian citizen. She was blessed with another baby boy and a girl, who were Canadians by birth.

AUTHOR'S BIOGRAPHY

Kass Ghayouri was born in Durban, South Africa, and immigrated to Canada in 1989. She graduated with a Bachelor of Arts Degree in English and Psychology. She attained a postgraduate degree in English, School Guidance, and Counseling. Her personality and passion shine through her years of experience as a twelfth-grade English teacher at a secondary school in Toronto. She patiently taught literature and writing skills to her academic English classes. In addition, she continues to have great influence and a substantial presence in the corporate world. Her success as a powerful businesswoman is evident in the tutorial school she and her husband own in Markham, Ontario, called **Governess Academy**. She is well known for her integrity, honesty, and passion as a teacher, businesswoman, talented artist, illustrator, poet, and author. She also tutors university students who face isolation and find the seminar experience a challenging learning environment.

Her novel *The Fugitive's Baby* has the potential to succeed on its own merits. It presents a captivating story that takes the reader on a rollercoaster ride, revealing deep-seated emotions. This novel documents the themes of love, romance, and fear, with articulate characters and a nostalgic plot. She has completed her second novel *An Era of Error.*

Made in the USA
Charleston, SC
19 June 2013